Moving Day

Written and illustrated by
CYNDY SZEKERES

A GOLDEN BOOK • NEW YORK

Western Publishing Company, Inc., Racine, Wisconsin 53404

It has been raining very hard
for a long time.
  The floor in the mouse house
is wet and muddy.

The leaf carpets are squooshy.

Water is plip-plopping
from the ceiling onto the table.

Father finds some dry leaves
for the floor. Mother clears the table.

The mice have a picnic underneath it.

Father says, "Everything is too wet!
It is time to move!"

Father and the little ones go out
to find a dry place to live.

After a short walk uphill,
the mice find lots of dry nooks and crannies
under the roots of a pine tree.
"This will be a good home," says Father.

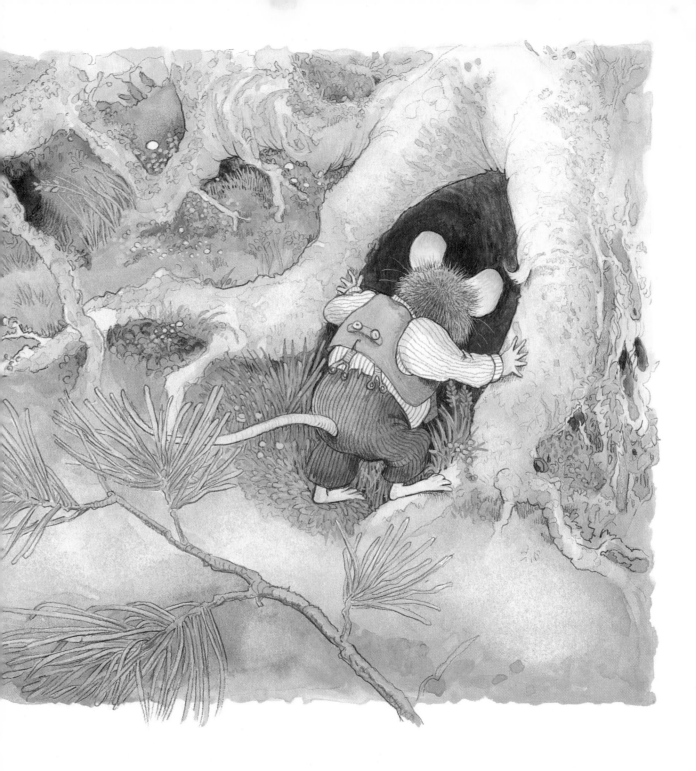

"But what will we cook with?" wails Sister.
"What will we play with?" whimpers Brother.
"Where will we sleep?" cries Tiny.

"We will go home
and pack all of our things
and move them up here," Father says.
They go home to do just that.

All of the mouse things
are stacked on a big fern. Big leaves
cover the furniture to keep it dry.

Little leaves keep each mouse dry.
It is easy to pull the fern over the wet,
slippery grass.

Under the tree on top of the hill
each mouse unpacks something,

except for Baby, who watches
from a new perch.

It is a fine new warm, dry
mouse house!

On the dry, sandy floor
the happy mice dance.